# EL NOMBRE

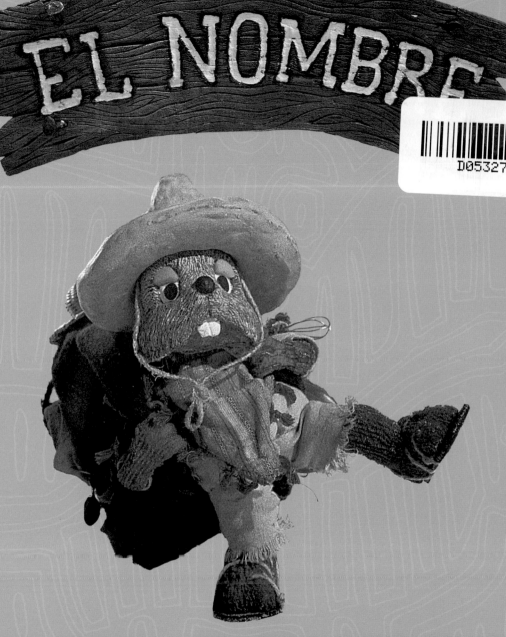

# The Great Train Robbery

## By Christopher Lillicrap

D0532711

"All aboard, all aboard," called Senor Loco as he pulled the train whistle.

Toot! Toot!

"Quickly Pedro," called Miss Constanza Bonanza, as Pedro jumped aboard the train. "The rest of the class are here. Do you know where Little Juan is? If he doesn't come soon he'll miss the train and he won't be able to come on the camping trip with us," she worried.

"There he is!" cried Pedro, pointing.

Little Juan was staggering down the street with a huge rucksack on his back.

"Wait for me, wait for me," Juan gasped.

"I'm sorry I'm late Miss Bonanza," he said, "but Mama packed so many things in my rucksack it's taken me ages to get here."

"We're only going for two days, not two weeks," called Pedro. All the children laughed as Little Juan clambered aboard.

**Toot! Toot!**

Senor Loco pulled the whistle again and the train began to move very slowly.

The children looked out of the window and saw Leonardo de Sombrero driving his pizza bike as fast as he could with Mama clinging onto the back.

"Stop the train!" called Mama. "Little Juan, you forgot your toothbrush," she shouted. Juan blushed and the other children giggled as the train came to a halt.

"I brought you a bowl of extra hot chilli with rice," Mama added. Everyone cheered because they all thought that Mama's extra hot chilli with rice was delicious.

"I think there is enough for all of you," said Mama as she passed the chilli through the carriage window to Juan.

"Wow, Mama," he said, "this smells really good."

Meanwhile, no one had noticed that the Wicked Don Fandango was hiding behind the station. "Mmmm! Mama's extra hot chilli with rice," he cried, sniffing the air. "It will soon be in the tummy of me, Don Fandango. Ah, ah, ahhhh!"

Don Fandango ran up to Senor Loco's cab.

"Help, help!" cried Senor Loco. But
the Wicked Don Fandango pulled
him off the train. Don Fandango took
the controls and the train slowly
set off again.

"Oh no, my train, my train,"
cried Senor Loco as the engine
pulled away.

Mama saw Don Fandango pull Senor Loco from the train. Quickly, she jumped onto the back of the moving carriage.

"Little Juan! Children! Are you all right?" cried Mama as the train got faster and faster.

"My poor class!" cried Constanza Bonanza. "How will we stop the train?"

"I don't know, but I know someone who does," said Little Juan.

# "Yes, it is I, El Nombre,"

El Nombre announced
as he swung to the rescue.

"So the chilli thief
has struck again,
And what is more,
he stole the train."

"Follow that train," El Nombre said as he jumped on the back of Leonardo's pizza bike. The pair raced off after the train.

"Faster Leonardo, faster," shouted El Nombre. They managed to catch up with the train. El Nombre made an almighty jump from the bike and managed to swing himself onto the roof of the carriage. The train sped on faster and faster.

El Nombre spotted a huge cactus coming his way and jumped over it just in time.

"So El Nombre," chuckled the Wicked Don Fandango, "try and stop me would you?"

"Oh no, Don Fandango," said El Nombre with a laugh, "this time I'm going to let you go."

"Let me go?" Don Fandango puzzled.

"Oh, yes," said El Nombre as he reached down and unhooked the engine from the carriage.

"Adios Amigo," El Nombre called as Don Fandango disappeared into the distance. El Nombre could just hear him shouting, "Where's the brake? Where's the brake?"

"Thank you, El Nombre," said Little Juan, "you saved us all."

"But how can we ever repay you?" asked Mama.

"Well. . ." said El Nombre looking at the bowl in Juan's hand.

"How about some of your extra hot chilli with rice?"

Mama gave El Nombre a bowl of her special extra hot chilli with rice.

"Wow!" said El Nombre going very red and spluttering, "that was very hot indeed."

"Adios Amigos and keep smiling!"

# EL NOMBRE'S PUZZLES

Help El Nombre save the day by working out these puzzles. You might need to go back and check the story to answer some of the questions.

◆ How many wheels does Leonardo's pizza bike have?

◆ How many of these pots of extra hot chilli with rice are empty?

◆ How many hats has Mama packed for Juan?

◆ This train has one engine. How many carriages does it have?

◆ Can you read this picture story? Count the little gerbils and work out the puzzle.

There are  in  class.

The  is taking them on a camping trip.

 have brought a  with them.

How many  don't have a  ?

**Answers** ◆ 2 wheels ◆ 3 empty pots ◆ 3 hats ◆ 2 carriages ◆ 3 gerbils don't have a tent.